Diana Stovin

However Did That Get There?

Bumblebee Books
London

BUMBLEBEE PAPERBACK EDITION

A CIP catalogue record for this title is
available from the British Library.

ISBN: 978-1-83934-490-9

Bumblebee Books is an imprint of
Olympia Publishers.

First Published in 2022

Bumblebee Books
Tallis House
2 Tallis Street
London
EC4Y 0AB

Printed in Great Britain

www.olympiapublishers.com

Dedication

I dedicate this book to the many children I taught.

Once upon a time there was a daddy mouse, a mummy mouse and a teeny, tiny baby mouse. Daddy Mouse was big and chubby with beady brown eyes and a set of whiskers to be proud of! Mummy Mouse was sleek and slender with kind brown eyes and whiskers always so neat and tidy.

Now, teeny, tiny Baby Mouse was not ready to be big and chubby or sleek and slender but his eyes were round and brown and his whiskers were growing very nicely.

The mouse family didn't live deep, down under the ground. They didn't live mid-way under the ground. They lived JUST under the ground so that they could peep out and sniff the air with their whiskers and watch the world with their beady, kind, round brown eyes.

In their home JUST under the ground everything was just as you would expect. There was a big chair for big, chubby Daddy Mouse.

There was a medium chair for sleek and slender Mummy Mouse and a little chair for teeny, tiny Baby Mouse.

Everything was spick and span with not a thing out of place.

They spent their days nibbling this and that, scurrying here and there to escape the heart-thumping pounce of the neighbourhood cat or just cuddling up snug and small in their spick and span home JUST under the ground.

So, imagine their surprise one day when something happened to disturb their spick and span home with not a thing out of place!

Something started to dangle through the roof of their home. Something thin and pointy, something dirty and brown, something flippy and floppy AND that something scattered soil all over their spick and span home JUST under the ground.

Daddy Mouse reached up on his hind legs to sniff at the flippy floppy something.

Teeny, tiny Baby Mouse scurried around nervously and excitedly.

Something was coming through the roof of their house!

Mummy Mouse just stared at the mess in their spick and span home.

Daddy, Mummy and
teeny, tiny Baby Mouse
stood stock still for
a moment, wondering if
something awful was about to
happen. Their whiskers began
to twitch rapidly, trying to
sense if danger was about.

Here a twitch, there a twitch,
everywhere a twitch, twitch - but
nothing dawned on them. Their beady,
brown eyes did not spy anything out of
order. Their noses did not sniff anything
out of order. Their ears did not hear
anything out of order and their sleek, brown fur did
not feel anything out of order.

After time had stood still for a very long time for teeny,
tiny Baby Mouse. Daddy Mouse said, "I think I had better go
and have a look outside."

Carefully, Daddy Mouse put his nose and whiskers just outside their home JUST under the ground. He couldn't see, hear, smell or feel anything out of order.

Bravely, he ventured out just a little bit further. Still no clues!

Looking to left and right and venturing ever further away from the safety of the entrance to their home, Daddy Mouse looked all around him.

It was getting gloomy, for it was getting late in the day, but Daddy Mouse could neither see nor hear anything out of order. Perhaps the flippy, floppy thing would go away in the night, perhaps everything would be spick and span in the morning.

"Yes," he told himself, "everything will be all right in the morning."

Daddy Mouse slipped carefully back inside his home JUST under the ground.

Mummy Mouse and teeny, tiny Baby Mouse were snuggled up closely to each other. It was a very comfortable snuggle up.

"There's nothing to see outside," said Daddy Mouse slowly as if to reassure himself as much as his family. By this time, Mummy Mouse had swept up the mess caused by the flippy, floppy thing and she was hoping it wasn't going to make any more mess!

It was hard to settle down to sleep that evening for the Mouse family. The flippy, floppy thing wasn't doing them any harm and, thankfully for Mummy Mouse, it wasn't making any more mess. It was just hanging there like an electric wire hangs from the ceilings in your houses with lampshades on the end.

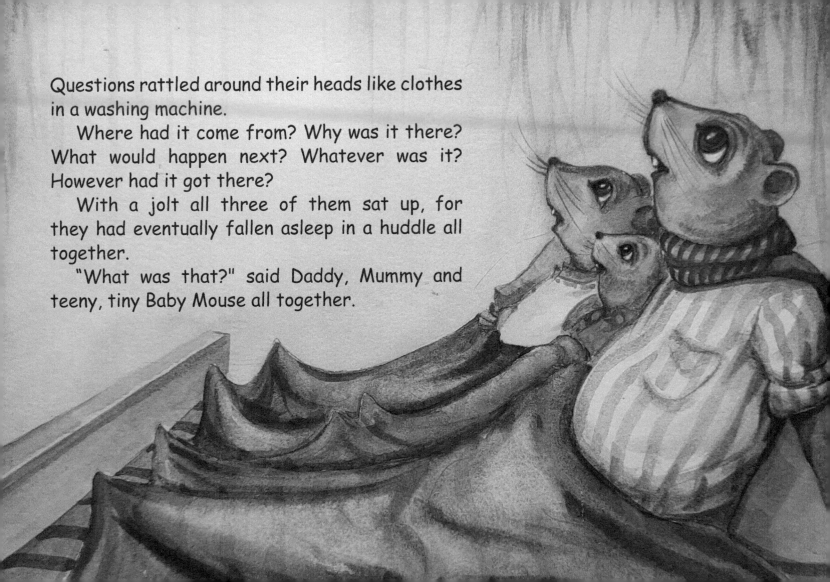

Questions rattled around their heads like clothes in a washing machine.

Where had it come from? Why was it there? What would happen next? Whatever was it? However had it got there?

With a jolt all three of them sat up, for they had eventually fallen asleep in a huddle all together.

"What was that?" said Daddy, Mummy and teeny, tiny Baby Mouse all together.

Their sleepy eyes lifted upwards to the roof of their spick and span home and there, before their startled eyes, was another flippy floppy thing!

ANOTHER FLIPPY, FLOPPY THING WAS DANGLING THROUGH THE ROOF!

Whatever should they do? Quick as a flash, Daddy Mouse zipped outside to see what was going on and instantly he knew what the flippy, floppy thing was!

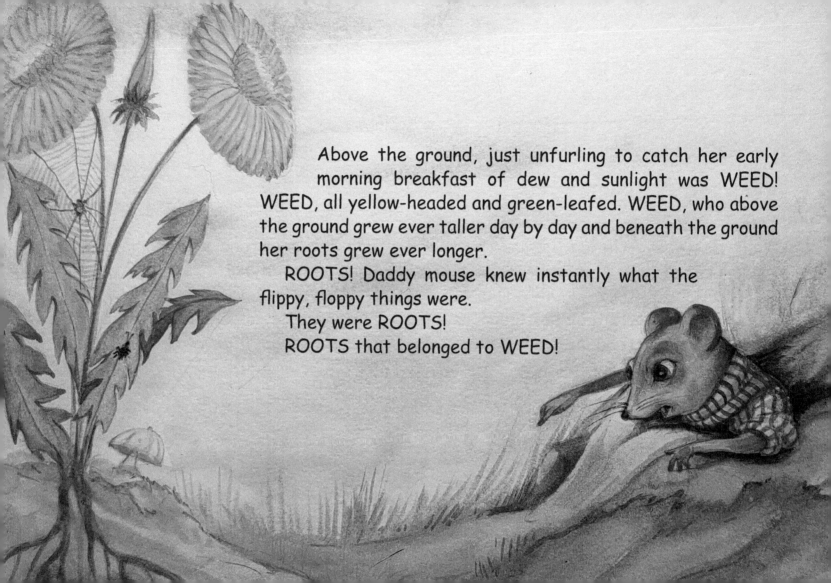

Above the ground, just unfurling to catch her early
morning breakfast of dew and sunlight was WEED!
WEED, all yellow-headed and green-leafed. WEED, who above
the ground grew ever taller day by day and beneath the ground
her roots grew ever longer.

ROOTS! Daddy mouse knew instantly what the
flippy, floppy things were.

They were ROOTS!

ROOTS that belonged to WEED!

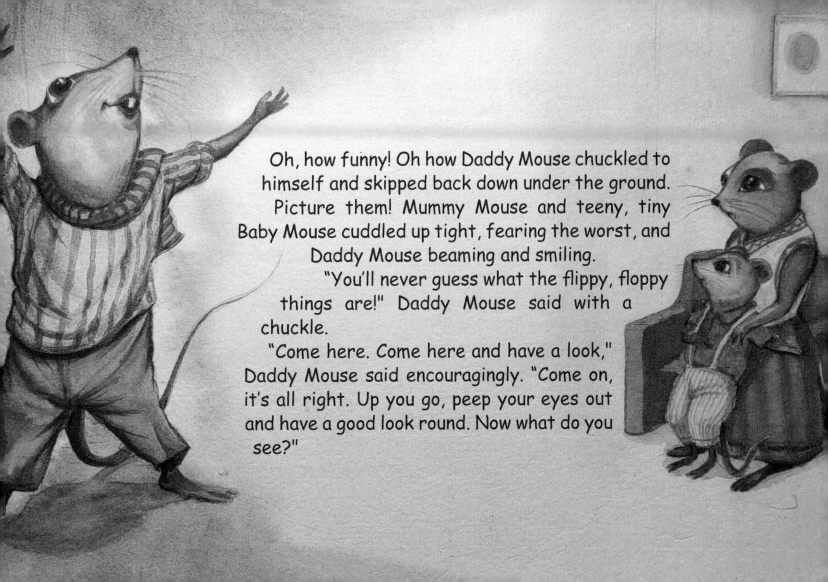

Oh, how funny! Oh how Daddy Mouse chuckled to himself and skipped back down under the ground. Picture them! Mummy Mouse and teeny, tiny Baby Mouse cuddled up tight, fearing the worst, and Daddy Mouse beaming and smiling.

"You'll never guess what the flippy, floppy things are!" Daddy Mouse said with a chuckle.

"Come here. Come here and have a look," Daddy Mouse said encouragingly. "Come on, it's all right. Up you go, peep your eyes out and have a good look round. Now what do you see?"

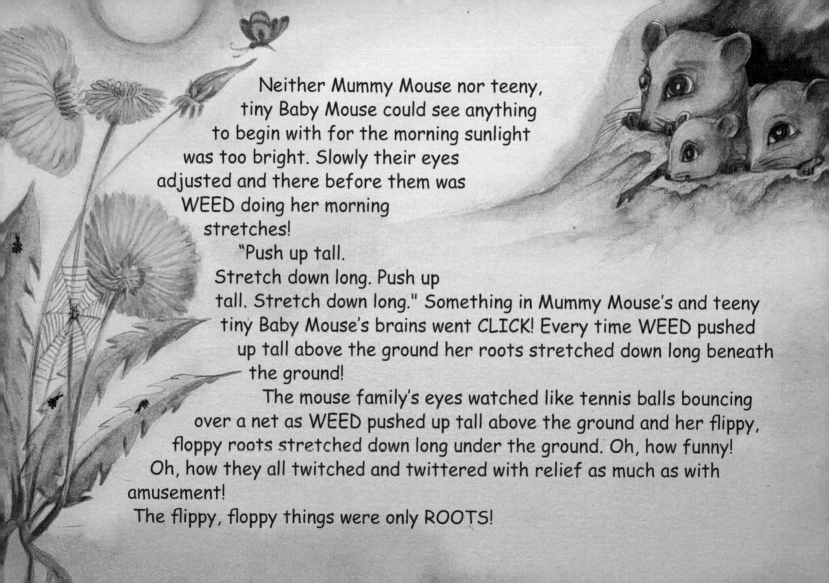

Neither Mummy Mouse nor teeny,
tiny Baby Mouse could see anything
to begin with for the morning sunlight
was too bright. Slowly their eyes
adjusted and there before them was
WEED doing her morning
stretches!
"Push up tall.
Stretch down long. Push up
tall. Stretch down long." Something in Mummy Mouse's and teeny
tiny Baby Mouse's brains went CLICK! Every time WEED pushed
up tall above the ground her roots stretched down long beneath
the ground!
The mouse family's eyes watched like tennis balls bouncing
over a net as WEED pushed up tall above the ground and her flippy,
floppy roots stretched down long under the ground. Oh, how funny!
Oh, how they all twitched and twittered with relief as much as with
amusement!
The flippy, floppy things were only ROOTS!

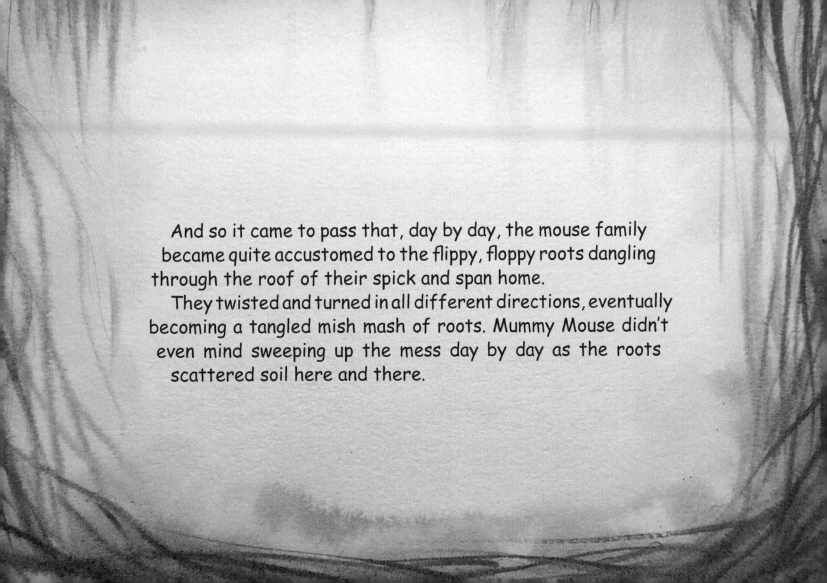

And so it came to pass that, day by day, the mouse family became quite accustomed to the flippy, floppy roots dangling through the roof of their spick and span home.

They twisted and turned in all different directions, eventually becoming a tangled mish mash of roots. Mummy Mouse didn't even mind sweeping up the mess day by day as the roots scattered soil here and there.

Now teeny, tiny Baby Mouse, who you remember was growing whiskers very nicely, had a very clever idea.

He was thinking one day of somewhere to keep his Sunday best drinking cup safe as he was no longer the smallest mouse around.

He looked all around: up, down, left and right and then his eyes fell upon the mish, mash of roots.

'Perfect!' he thought. He threaded one of the flippy, floppy roots through the handle of his cup. It fitted perfectly and was safe and sound out of harm's way until Sunday came around again and he would be allowed blackberry juice in his best drinking cup.

"What a clever idea!" said Daddy Mouse as his mind wandered over the fright that the flippy, floppy things had given them when they first appeared in their spick and span home JUST under the ground.

Time passed on and the mouse family grew bigger and had to move to another home JUST under the ground.

All their belongings moved with them, apart from teeny, tiny Baby Mouse's Sunday best drinking cup. He left it safely threaded on to the flippy, floppy root because it was safe there and he felt safe again.

WEED enjoyed the long days of summer sun upon her ever-stretching tall self, but, as the cooler days of autumn began to arrive, WEED began to wither and shrivel into the ground. Very soon she began to feel herself being shivered and shaken from the soil around her. Her roots were being gently eased out of the ground and curious eyes were looking at her and saying, "However did that get there?"

I wonder...

About the Author

I wrote *However did that get there?* soon after I retired as an infant school teacher. The inspiration came from the many years of reading stories to the children which I always considered to be the happiest part of the day.

Acknowledgements

My family and friends did not know for a long time that I had written the story! A friend and family members initially did the illustrations and printed it and it was their encouragement that led me to submit it to a publisher. Thank you to Tony and Sarah Lawn for their printing skills. Thank you to Sarah Perks for the fun and laughter in having a go at the illustrations. Thank you to Olympia Publishers for their support and interest in publishing this book.